the pastor

A CRISIS

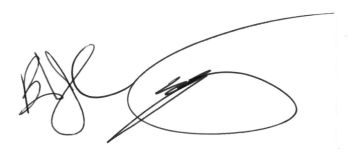

The Pastor

THE PASTOR: a crisis

This is a work of fiction. Names, characters, places and
events in this novel are products of the authors' imagina-
tions or fictionalized composites of real events and people
(with their permission).

"The Sojourn" is adapted from a poem by Dominic Jersak.

Cover design: Bruce Gore www.gorestudioinc@gmail.com

Printed in Altona, Canada by Friesens Corporation.

ISBN: 978-1-7327417-5-1
Library of Congress Control Number:
2020908995

The Pastor
a crisis

Bradley Jersak
& Paul Young

Cappella
Books

Nashville, Tennessee

For Jacki

The mind is its own place,
and in itself can make a heaven of hell,
a hell of heaven.

— John Milton, *Paradise Lost*

To close ourselves to others in hardness of heart, and
to live with clenched fists, would surely mean not liv-
ing at all anymore. It would mean being buried alive.

— Jürgen Moltmann

the Patient

Nothing can separate us from the love and presence of God, but we can live—now and in eternity—as if God is not present, as if God does not exist or love us. And that is the definition of hell.

—Kenneth Tanner

God sees. He sees the truth, but he waits.

—Tolstoy

THE PATIENT CLENCHES HIS FIST, rolling it over and giving it a hard stare from every angle. Clench. Unclench. Clenching again, jaw and temples unconsciously mimicking the contractions. He fixates on cracked, white skin tightening over his knuckles, pulsing blue veins swelling proudly across the back of his hand.

A kaleidoscopic flash of news images from his youth. The raised fists of Revolution. Black Panthers, Marxist university students, his father. *Whoever.*

"Whomever," the internal critic nags, that proverbial pickle residing in his butt. *"Yes, whomever!"* It echoes off the bare walls of his inside world, while outside he sits tight-knuckled in defiance, another sea of unremarkable faces cascading in front of him like a slow motion waterfall, the wannabes he once needed (but no one who can tell him that).

"Those willful bastards, leeching whiners, all hypocrites!" He seethes and then snickers through constricted nostrils as if there might still be an audience.

So, why the crooked smirk? Maybe it's the wry irony that it's he who's landed here instead of those parasitic "them." *He* is nothing like *them.* And *now* is nothing like *then.*

A flash of some insipid televised pop shrink telling everyone that bruised hearts cower within the angry fist. Or one of those clever mockumentaries highlighting the desperate resolve that finally ignites a rural Muslim, a bullied middle-schooler, a battered housewife—perhaps, even a respected Pastor—to take matters into their own formerly gentle hands.

He contemplates hands, all sorts of hands. Hands overturning clay for garden plots, hands writing furtive love notes in the lunchroom, hands kneading dough or anointing with oil. Fists now . . . squeezing a pipe bomb or a paring knife. Whatever it takes. Whatever's at hand. Whatever the bravado one's violent fantasies might muster. *"Whatever!"*

He snorts. Bizarre. The helpless folly of it all. We ignorantly, or worse, with good intention make vows that force these hands to trigger a chaotic series of self-defeating inevitabilities. *"Lustily addicted to that precious self-destruct button, aren't we?"* Somewhere else, at this very moment, a would-be hero blows off his own hands, and a cornered victim slices through her own eighteen- or eighty-eight-year-old arteries. *"Sick!"*

"She swallowed the spider to catch the fly," he mutters, the tune barely audible through clenched teeth "I guess she'll die." *"Oooh, yeah,"* the patient thinks in his creepiest villain vibrato, *"they're a-a-a-all supposed to die."*

Well, it hadn't worked out that way, and it was his own damn fault.

His mind darts to Homer's *Iliad*. The "poem of force." The patient had read half *The Iliad* once, on his smartphone. Now what was its point? Ah yes, when we try to use force, it turns on us, and then possesses us for its own ends. Then we're truly and utterly screwed.

What struck him, oddly, in this moment, was that Homer coined the phrase "bit the dust." And so, they did. Fickle gods manipulating self-centered "heroes" into killing each other. How bloody noble. No, really, they actually thought so!

"But then, so do we," the patient sermonizes in his head. *"For the grandest of ideals, we still offer our children to insatiable gods. Whether it's Molech and Mars, or Stars and Stripes, our sons and daughters are strewn across the globe in the cause of "freedom."* If only they weren't too dead to enjoy it.

Although it is so easy, it is too simplistic to point the accusatory finger of blame, but in his current state, our patient no longer knows better. Confronted by his own projections and internal enemies, he'd rather stay in denial than actually face them. The irony is now his façade itself is raising an allegation. Like a prosecuting attorney it declares to him that his own moral outrage at the world is a form of confession, and all of it triggered by "the visitor." So, that jaded wry smirk is really pointed inward. This he might acknowledge on a saner and more honest day—which is to say, ever more rarely.

The patient knows all about noble and good intentions. Hell, a noble intention to force God's hand was the rope that hung Judas, right? *Hmph.* So, why that smug, cynical but crooked smile? Ah, there it is: bitterness.

He again admires his clenched fist: such a beautiful emblem of initiative, boldness, and courage. AKA, *"charging blindly out of the foxhole into certain death."* But isn't that precisely how fists work?

Grasping, clinging, scheming. Manipulating, mastering, making. Taking, demanding, working. Striving, driving, crashing, burning—

Shut up! a voice screams inside, but barely escapes the gritted teeth.

Damned voices! But he both needs and disdains his unspoken vows of silence. "Shhh!"

"Better not look there. Think about "them," about my people, about that intruder."

The kettle comes to a boil, and he can't help himself.

"If God won't do something, I WILL!"

"Crap!" For God's sake, keep it inside!

The orderly, wearing her childish smock patterned with teddy bears, glances at the patient and glides over. She crouches beside him and, with saccharine tones, coaxes open his frozen fist.

"Sir? Er, Pastor?"

"Yes, that's right: Pastor . . . the Bible-wavin', stage-struttin' glory days."

"Pastor, we haven't taken our meds yet, have we? Let me help you."

"Yes, choke down this bitter pill."

"Thanks, Mary Poppins," he says, leering as she bends in close. "Yesiree, a spoonful of sugar helps the medicine go down." He senses her shudder.

Then, finally, good old Morpheus beckons him to some deep zees.

ACROSS THE ROOM on his own gurney, behind chestnut eyes and brambles of a tarnished silver beard a one-handed mute ponders the Pastor. Cross-legged, he rocks to and fro in swaddling sheets, humming a repetitive refrain. The knobby digits of his remaining hand are tangled with "worry beads," and those ancient eyes never leave the other man.

"Holy fool," the Pastor judges as he begins to doze.

Oddly, unanticipated notes of consolation wash over him in rhythm with the vagabond's muttering and motion—strangely soothing.

Patients. Patience.

COLLAPSE

Police Report

The Pastor was real agitated this morning, all through pre-service prayer, right from the get-go. There's the stuff we know and the stuff we don't know. The stuff we know is tense enough, but there's also a whole lot going on "back o' the kitchen," so to say.

Everyone's been feeling it. Pacing his study like a cage, like a tiger at the zoo marking his territory. Small wonder considering the sermon he let loose. Went off like a volcano. Classic hellfire and brimstone, going off like he does sometimes, but this was over the top. Total cringe factor. I mean, he started with holiness and all, but it got deep into fear and hate in no time.

The hate started with faraway targets—the Russians, the Muslims—then circled closer: the gays, the liberals, the hypocrites. But soon it felt like he was hating on us. Or maybe himself. By now he's all red and sweaty and hollering. More than usual, I mean.

So, he's really getting down to it. And just then, this stranger comes in, pretty late. A visitor. Never saw her before. Would've remembered—a bit of a cougar, I'd say. Tall, pretty, dark. More of a power suit than we're used to, and hair cut shorter than Pastor would usually approve. I was in the choir, so I saw the whole thing. Really, everyone must've. She comes up the aisle right to the front pew, right to the 'reserved section' and sits down. And dark eyes. Dark like daggers.

So anyway, Pastor doesn't notice right away, because he's pretty much caught up in the Spirit. But then she laughed—or maybe snorted—and he sees her. He sees her, and she totally triggers him. He pulls up short and stops and spins 'round, so the choir can see his face full on. Lordy, he turns from beet red to blue to white to death gray in a few seconds. Eyes get real big, and then they start rolling back all creepy. But he doesn't go down. No, he starts grabbing at his throat and pulling open his tie. Then he's tearing open his shirt. Buttons are popping, and he's clawing at his chest. Scared the bejesus outta me. I was sure he was stroking out. Sounds nuts, but that's when it starts to get really weird!

He's taking his suit off. I mean, all of it! Like it's burning him. Like he's on fire from the inside. And now he's all red again, and his chest is bleeding, and he's moaning, only higher pitched. And by the time he drops his drawers, me and the other deacons are hauling him down. Jay is calling 911, and Pastor's wife is shrieking, and then the cops come, and Pastor's freaking and flailing till they finally zap him. 'Scuse my French, but where I grew up, we call that batshit crazy.

Strangest thing though. The visitor just sat there all calm. And she's got this little smile. Like the Mona Lisa, you know? As eerie as Pastor, now that I think of it. Like, who was she? Why was she there? What is she to him? And then she's just gone. Like she dissolved into thin air or crawled back into her hole.

City Police Report: Central Precinct
Eyewitness Statement 2
Transcript: Pastor's Wife

No, nothing like this has ever happened before. My husband has always been in charge. In control. Sure, sometimes he has a temper, but he almost never gets violent. Not for a long time anyway. He does get animated when it comes to preaching or business meetings or football, but he says it's always strategic or tactical, like he's aiming it. He hardly ever aims it at me, and he's really good at managing it.

"Quarterbacking the spirit" he calls it.

But today was totally out of character. He never,

ever acted like that before. He had always been able to hold it in.

I suppose something was building. He hasn't been sleeping well for five or maybe six months now. Not proper sleep anyway. I'm guessing maybe three hours a night? It's like he was running from the nightmares. Most nights he was twitchy and cried in his sleep a lot. But he never talked about the dreams. He's private that way, even with me. If I asked, he'd just go quiet or lock himself in his study or say, "Don't go there," and I knew he meant it.

The longer that went on, the more his preaching got that way. My husband truly is a loving man, and charming. But yes, the sermons got meaner. He called it conviction, but it was like when he was awake, he was chasing what chased him in the night.

I don't know who she was, but when the visitor appeared, he acted like the nightmare had come alive in this world. Took on a life of its own and turned on him. Like she was a demon sent to drag him down into hell. Oh God, I hope he can find his way back.

But back to what? I mean, after that? We'll never be able to show our faces here again. What will people think? How do you move past something like that?

Intake

St. Macrina's Hospital:
Psychiatric Wing
Admissions Summary

Date of Admission: 04-04
Patient: The Pastor   **Date of Birth:** 11-01-58

04-01   1130 – ER Intake: Patient was delivered in restraints to ER via ambulance. Paramedics summoned by police following Taser incident, First Baptist Church. Patient had stripped naked and was raging. Catatonic on arrival at hospital.

Male. Date of birth: 11-01-1958.

04-03   0530 – Patient regains partial consciousness after 52 hours. Violent thrashing against restraints.

Non-verbal vocalizing and mixture of religious expletives and profanity. Sedatives prescribed.

Collapses into unconsciousness.

04-03 .1630 – Patient half-awake, shrieking religious themes: "fire, hell, Jesus." Exhausted, fitful sleep.
04-04 0800 – Patient regains consciousness. Vital signs stable but turned inward, mumbling to himself. Appears to be arguing. Severe derealization.
See Admissions Mental Status Exam 04-04.

~ ~ ~

Admissions Mental Status Exam

Date of Admission: 04-04
Client: The Pastor   **Date of Birth:** 11-01-58

OBSERVATIONS

Appearance

☐ Neat   ☑ Disheveled   ☑ Inappropriate

☑ Bizarre   ☐ Other

Speech

☐ Normal   ☐ Tangential   ☑ Pressured

☐ Impoverished   ☐ Other

Eye Contact

☐ Normal   ☑ Intense   ☑ Avoidant

Motor Activity

☐ Normal ☑ Restless ☑ Tics ☐ Slowed

Affect

☐ Full ☑ Constricted ☐ Flat ☐ Labile

Comments: *Patient is turned inward. No sign of connection to outer world. Able to speak (mumbling to himself). Very intense, muttering accusatory words ("hypocrite," "bastards"); aggressive but directed exclusively inwards.*

MOOD

☐ Euthemic ☑ Anxious ☑ Angry ☐ Depressed
☐ Euphoric ☑ Irritable ☐ Other

COGNITION

Orientation Impairment

☐ None ☑ Place ☑ Object ☐ Person
☑ Time

Memory Impairment

☐ None ☑ Short-term ☐ Long-term ☑ Other

Attention

☐ Normal ☑ Distracted ☑ Other

Comments: *No sense of time or place. Would assume he is disconnected entirely from this world except for verbal triggers and compulsive nervous glances and glares at "Patient Max."*

PERCEPTION

Hallucinations

☐ None ☑ Auditory ☐ Visual

Other

☐ None ☑ Derealization ☐ Depersonalization

Comments: *In conversation with himself and/or possibly an imaginary second party who seems to speak in first person to the patient.*

THOUGHTS

Suicidality

☑ None ☐ Ideation ☐ Plain ☐ Intent

Homicidality

☑ None ☐ Aggressive ☐ Intent ☐ Plan

Delusions

☐ None ☐ Grandiose ☑ Paranoid ☑ Religious

Comments: *Patient's aggression is entirely self-focused, but while extremely accusatory, no evidence of physical self-harm or suicidal gestures. The majority of verbals have religious overtones.*

BEHAVIOR

☐ Cooperative ☑ Guarded ☐ Hyperactive

☑ Agitated   ☐ Paranoid   ☐ Stereotyped
☐ Aggressive   ☑ Bizarre   ☑ Withdrawn

Comments: *Behavior is extremely agitated but non-threatening to others. Whatever connection there is to the outside world seems fearful.*

INSIGHTS

☐ Good   ☐ Fair   ☑ Poor

Comments: *Significant delusion.*

JUDGMENT

☐ Good   ☐ Fair   ☑ Poor

Comments: *Incapacitated.*

04-04 1600 – Unresponsive to neurologist.
EEG ordered.

04-05 1600 – Psych Ward Admission. EEG results: Epilepsy ruled out. Preliminary diagnosis: stress or trauma-related dissociative state. Admitted to psychiatric ward for further evaluation. See MMSE 04-06.

PSYCH MMSE
(Mini Mental Status Exam)
Attending Physician: Dr. Angelica Hope

Date: 04-06
Client: The Pastor   **Date of Birth:** 11-01-58

One point for each answer

ORIENTATION: Ask the patient time and location.

Year Season Month Date Time	0/5
Country Town District Hospital Ward Floor	0/5

Comments: *Patient responded to each time question, "Time is ticking," not as answers but triggered by each question as if a third party was addressing him. Tone was threatening. Patient responded to location questions in same manner: "Into the pit. Through the gates."*

REGISTRATION: Examiner names 3 objects (apple, table, penny) and asks the patient to repeat (1 point for each correct). Then the patient learns the 3 names, repeating until correct.   **0/3**

Comments: *Patient didn't respond by repeating but again was triggered by the words to word association. To "apple" with "Eden," to "table" with "stab it" and "can't kill the beast," to "penny" with "whose image is this?"*

ATTENTION: Subtract 7 from 100, then repeat from result. Continue five times: 100, 93, 86, 79, 65.
Alternative: spell "WORLD" backwards.

| 0/5 |

Comments: *No response to the numbers test. To "spell world backwards" again triggered to possible word association [?]: "decreation."*

RECALL: Ask for the names of the three objects learned earlier. [no response]

| 0/3 |

LANGUAGE: Name two objects (pen, watch). [no response]

| 0/2 |

Repeat "No ifs, ands, or buts." [no response]

| 0/1 |

Give a three-stage command. Score 1 for each stage. ("Place index finger of right hand on your nose and then on your left ear.")

| 1/3 |

Comments: *Until now, no eye contact. When given this command, there was a dark, direct glare with eye contact. The patient used the index finger of his right hand but pointed it like a gun to his forehead.*

Ask the patient to read and obey a written command on a piece of paper. (Instruction: "Close your eyes.")

| 0/1 |

Comments: *Patient's eyes indicated some recognition of what he read. Note: Immediate rapid eye movement*

Ask the patient to write a sentence. Score 1 if it is sensible and has a subject and a verb.

1/1

Comments: *Patient wrote, "Abandon all hope, ye who enter here."*

COPYING: Ask the patient to copy a pair of intersecting pentagrams.

0/1

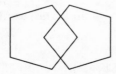

Comments: *Objects such as pencils deemed unsafe for patient.*

MMSE scoring total:

2/30

24–30: no cognitive impairment
18–23: mild cognitive impairment
0–17: severe cognitive impairment

Comments: *The patient can hear external voices, but rather than responding directly, he consistently reacts with word associations similar to autistic triggering. Severe derealization—incorporates stimuli as his own ideations into his alternative mental world. This world appears to involve a second voice that sometimes speaks aloud in first person to the patient.*

Max

HIS CLENCHED FIST was still pumping, forcing scabs on the Pastor's knuckles to crack open. A watery ooze seeped from his wounds. He couldn't help tonguing the tender sores, but at least he refrained from picking, for now. Best to leave God's bandages in place to ward off infection. That was more self-control than he'd shown when he first inflicted the injury. But at least the unpatched holes in the ward wall proved he got the better of that outburst—left his mark.

The orderlies were grateful when he'd directed his blows toward inert plaster. But with the way Max kept eyeing him, it was just luck—*holy luck*—that the Pastor hadn't socked him, socked him royally in that ugly mute mouth.

"Idiot," the Pastor rumbled to himself. *"And what's with that missing hand? And the nosey stares?"*

Furtive peeks at Max's chart offered no clues to who he was or why he was admitted—nothing beyond his first name and intake date (the same as the Pastor's, coincidentally). Confidentiality, you say? That's just wrong. Wasn't he entitled to know who this nutter was sleeping in the bed next to him? Could be a psycho murderer, for all he knew.

Even Max's nightstand drawer was locked. The Pastor had checked. Sure enough. What do they say? It's not paranoia if they really are out to get you. Ironic but apropos in this case, don't you think?

That the Pastor would ponder anyone beyond himself was somewhat of a breakthrough. A brief foray outside the walls of his narcissism. Curiosity teased it out of him. He had questions. And theories, and Max was an easy target. What act of insanity had landed him there? And how had the old dog managed to lose a paw? Crushed in a machine press? A bandsaw accident? Building a bomb? Yes, the creases in his face marked Max as a tradesman. Not bright enough to be white collar. But really, hardly a skilled carpenter with an injury like that. Was Max someone else's awkward laborer or the failed ending of a father-son business?

"Two left thumbs soon lead to just one thumb total," he sneered to himself.

In another time—in the brighter days and better lands of God's righteous Law: eye-for-an-eye, tooth-for-a-tooth justice—he could assume Max was a thief whose hand had been caught in the cookie jar. A missing limb meant justice had been served. Not like these wretched days of liberal lawyers and legal loopholes. Gone were the days of "three strikes and you're incarcerated." Now even capital punishment was under constant threat. Sheer barbarism.

"Where's the outrage?" he demanded to no one in particular. God didn't seem to be on the line. "Where's the outrage?" he asked again, this time out loud in Max's general direction.

Not that the Pastor was bloodthirsty—no. No, but who took sin seriously anymore? Cheap grace, soft on sin: the bane of secure Christian democracy, a red carpet for the hordes of hell to overrun the nation. And so, they had.

Vengeance belongs to the Lord (all too slowly, in the Pastor's opinion), so he would leave the sword in the hands of the Almighty (his Second Amendment rights notwithstanding).

But the Pastor fancied himself a "preacher of righteousness," like Noah. The only real difference being now it was "turn or burn" rather than "turn or drown." A good dose of hellfire was desperately needed, so he preached to singe hearts rather than tickle the ears.

Popular? No, but the truth is a sword, right? Spiritual medicine often comes as a bitter pill, and soul surgery cuts deep. It's a moral necessity for the faithful. But don't shoot the doctor when he diagnoses your malady and prescribes the cure. He's doing you a solid. Enough people knew that to keep the Pastor busy.

Since his arrival, the Pastor had been biding his time and gathering his thoughts. Waiting for a sign— a prompting—before delivering his pent-up prognoses to this sorry lot. Including Max. And that quack of a psychiatrist.

Which is to say, the Pastor's newfound outward attention arose largely because he was ardently averting his mental gaze from the events that led him here. He needed to get his head together—to regain control—and this was proving difficult. *"Gather your thoughts, man. Sort yourself out."*

Hope

PSYCH MMSE
(Mini Mental Status Exam)
Attending Physician: Dr. Angelica Hope

Date: 04-20
Client: The Pastor   **Date of Birth:** 11-01-58

One point for each answer

ORIENTATION: Ask the patient time and location.

Year Season Month Date Time

| 1/5 |

Country Town District Hospital Ward Floor

| 3/5 |

Comments: *Patient was aware, but his responses were cryptic and apocalyptic. He knew the year but when asked for the season, he said, "The end of the end times." Perhaps more sarcastic than delusional, implying it as a warning for me.*

Patient knew city, town, and district, but when asked re: the hospital, said, "Sheol, Hades, Gehenna, Tartarus" [religious references?]. Then he laughed as if kidding and said, "The Hotel California, of course. Where else?" And then sang, "You can check out any time you like, but you can never leave."

REGISTRATION: Examiner names 3 objects (apple, table, penny) and asks the patient to repeat (1 point for each correct). Then the patient learns the 3 names, repeating until correct.

| 3/3 |

Comments: *Impatience growing. Before I could ask, responded, "Apple, table, coin. Next?" all at once.*

ATTENTION: Subtract 7 from 100, then repeat from result. Continue five times: 100, 93, 86, 79, 65.
Alternative: spell "WORLD" backwards.

| 4/5 |

Comments: *Quick response to the numbers test: "100, 93, 86, 79,65" quickly and all at once. To "spell world backwards," see previous word association, "decreation" backwards: "noitaerced."*

RECALL: Ask for the names of the three objects learned earlier.

| 3/3 |

LANGUAGE: Name two objects (pen, watch). [no response]

| 0/2 |

Repeat "No ifs, ands, or buts." | 0/1

Comments: *Sarcastic response: "Certitude. It's the chess players, not the artists, who can't get their heads around heaven and go mad." Worrisome similarity to Charles Manson interviews.]*

Give a three-stage command. Score 1 for each stage. ("Place index finger of right hand on your nose and then on your left ear.") | 1/3

Comments: *The patient pointed two fingers to his eyes, then to me, as in, "I'm watching you."*

Ask the patient to read and obey a written command on a piece of paper. (Instruction: "Close your eyes.") | 0/1

Comments: *The patient closed his eyes. Note: Entered rapid eye movement and hummed a tune..*

Ask the patient to write a sentence. Score 1 if it is sensible and has a subject and a verb. | 1/1

Comments: *Patient wrote the same phrase as before, "Abandon all hope, ye who enter here." [Discovered since to be from Dante's "Inferno."]*

COPYING: Ask the patient to copy a pair of intersecting pentagrams.

0/1

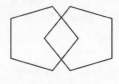 

Comments: *Patient was deliberate and focused. Drew the same picture but on his hand rather than on the paper. Pressure he applied looked painfully hard.*

MMSE scoring total:

16/30

24–30: no cognitive impairment
18–23: mild cognitive impairment
0–17: severe cognitive impairment

Comments: *The patient still seems to hear voices, but now they are more obviously internalized. Interaction is possible, but it's difficult to tell whether he's confused or uncooperative. The sarcasm and somewhat manic nature of his responses exudes aggression.*

Psychiatric Assessment
Attending Physician: Dr. Angelica Hope

Date: 04-20
Client: The Pastor   **Date of Birth:**11-01-58

04-20 The patient ("the Pastor") has progressed steadily since admission.

Has advanced from near catatonia to full consciousness.

Has shifted attention from nearly 100% inward focus to awareness of surroundings and people.

Has developed reactions from inner voices to external stimuli.

With his outer focus, the Pastor's general agitation has occasionally turned to aggression and outbursts. Orderlies have had to restrain and sedate him on a number of occasions, most recently after he punched a hole in the wall. I prefer not to isolate him, because his interactivity signals a significant shift beyond his mental imprisonment.

However, this interactivity may amount to or include acute projections of inner turmoil (shame? self-hatred?) from which the patient is fleeing to reinforce denial (from whatever secrets he wants to keep buried). Nevertheless, the Pastor exercises choices in acting out (indicating a measure of control that we want to encourage). For example, he knows to punch walls rather than people.

I will attempt a 1-on-1 interview before introducing him to a group therapy session.

THE WARD

Interview

ANGELICA HOPE (MD, DO) WELCOMED the Pastor into the ward interview room. The office at her private clinic was warmer and more luxurious, but at the hospital, she was happy enough to work with two facing chairs in a sunlit room. It was just spacious enough to include an inconspicuous (but watchful) orderly and a small round table (for note taking and assessments). Recessed into the wall was a large fish tank, home to a handful of shy tropical fish. The atmosphere quietly suggested help and hope to the hopeless.

Anyone who had the privilege of experiencing Dr. Hope's care would say she was a great physician, expertly assigning medication as needed but never in excess. More than that, she was a wonderful counselor—one might say supernaturally tender—but also incisive, able to glide gracefully past denial and defensiveness to the heart of the matter. Those in the know admired her aptitude for blending compassion with a cocktail of therapies for the healing of memories. Even then, the results defied explanation, though it must be admitted, healing and transformation require willingness on the part of the patient. Surrender can never be coerced, so Dr. Hope is patient, giving her clients over to a process that takes time, marked by great struggle and even pain. It wasn't uncommon for patients to beg her, "Just fix me!" And her reply was consistent: "I'm going as fast as you are able." For the stubborn and defiant, that was a hard truth but a truth nonetheless.

The Pastor took his chair, comfortable and thoughtfully placed to honor personal space without alienating the client, even at a slight angle that made eye contact possible while allowing patients freedom to glance away or reflect on the aquarium without awkwardness.

The good doctor quickly read the Pastor's body language: distrust, defensiveness, the need for control. His clenched fists spoke to her of willfulness—unsurprising for a man whose identity was bound up in— addicted to—conveying a charismatic presence and religious authority. But Dr. Hope could also see how his hands held invisible shields, deflecting reminders of the incident, the trigger, and the unique mixture of belief systems and secrets behind them.

Resisting that energy would only feed it.

To welcome the Pastor out of his prison, Dr. Hope needed to begin by granting some leeway, assurance that she wasn't about to try wrestling control from him. In time, the pain would do its own work. When at last he could face the shadows in his heart and mind, he *may* even allow the truth to walk him through the brokenness that leads to surrender and willingness. "May," because not all did. In her care, it was possible. In truth, the entire process was a healing journey, from beginning to end—even the "dark night"—but best seen in retrospect.

And so they began.

"Pastor . . . may I call you Pastor?"

Immediate effect. His identity had not and would not be stripped or stolen from him. He was prepared to fight for it, but there was no fight. This was disorienting, because it deprived him of the charged lecture he had prepared in defense of his hard-fought position and title. He thought about delivering his carefully prepared speech. He had so hoped it would consume the space of their session.

But for the first time—maybe in years—the Pastor conceded to something. A *very* small something when we realize he only conceded to her willingness to freely give what he had sought to demand. But let us not despise small beginnings. Even the smallest seeds can crack concrete, can they not?

"Yes." The last word he imagined saying at any point in the interview. The word he vowed would not pass his lips. "Yes, you may. And shall I call you *doctor*?" He was still spoiling for a fight—about what it was and why it was she had presumed to summoned him there.

She surprised him again, by neither playing down the role (which would have been a lie) nor holding it over him (I'm *your* doctor. I will *help* you). Instead, wisdom spoke through her. "As one professional to another, that seems fair. Yes, thank you." It was as if she were consenting to a good idea that he had proposed, a favor he was offering.

She followed up immediately with, "Pastor, what needs to happen here?" not "How can I *help* you?" or "Here's your problem" or "What's your problem?" She was asking him to do what he did best: give advice, offer opinions, make judgments. Asked directly for an agenda, the Pastor's constant need to bring one—and he had—was momentarily lost to him. The light-headedness that hit him was apparent to Dr. Hope, but she dared not offer any aid that would spotlight his weakness or need. She saw . . . and waited. Strangely, he felt honored by it. He even felt an inkling of respect for her silence. It fortified him with enough ego strength to reestablish his defenses. Others might have pounced on that moment. Dr. Hope did not. Patience, not pressure, would bear fruit in time.

"I think you should *listen* to me!" Even to him it felt a little loud, a little desperate, a little preachy. But once again, she did not call him on it.

"What do you sense I need to hear?"

Here was an educated woman—a fellow professional—willing to listen? Not, "What do you need to say?" or "What do you need to get off your chest?" (condescending), nor the challenge he so often faced from his opponents, "Well, you should listen to me!" It was as if she were genuinely looking for his input. Maybe she *needed* to hear what he had to say.

So, he told her. Nothing of his secrets (those were buried too deep for him to access), nor anything of the incident or the visitor who triggered it. No, for the rest of their hour, the good doctor listened to him—*attentively* listened—to him preach. He condemned the perversity of the world, preached against the lukewarm faith of the anemic church, lamented the lack of outrage against the debauchery of pagans and the fanaticism of false religions. He laid out his own apocalyptic vision, and on that foundation, he uttered an *anointed call* (if he did say so himself) for repentance and holiness in the face of divine judgment.

In short, the Pastor unloaded his entire belief system in an hour. Okay, to be honest, it was (as it was every Sunday) well over an hour. She hadn't shouted, "Amen!", but neither had she stomped out or cut him off with, "That's all for today." She had truly paid attention, never checked her watch, and took copious notes. He had snuck looks at her notes too. She wasn't writing things *about* him—things a doctor might say. She was honestly taking notes, taking interest.

He wasn't at all ready to trust his heart to her. Such private matters were best left that way. But he knew of no reason to keep his beliefs from her. He preached this message week after week to congregants, podcast subscribers, and even folks on the radio. Her reaction—non-judgmental listening and even some sincere nods—was a first step on the long walk home.

As Dr. Hope dismissed him, she said, "Thank you, Pastor. It's very clear to me now why you were such a well-respected gospel preacher."

The Pastor received the compliment cautiously.

"I understand that 'gospel' literally means 'good news,'" she added. "When we meet again, I'd very much like to hear your take on the perennial question: In light of the social ills you address, what is the *good* news?"

The Pastor's face turned to ice. Was it her first mistake of the session? One step too far?

"Screw you, Doctor," he answered with a venomous tone. He stood up and stomped out, slamming the door behind him.

Even the Pastor knew one had to walk through the shadow of the valley of death before the dawn broke.

Dr. Hope knew this too. She had not made a mistake. Her task was not to keep him happy or make him like her. After all, she was a doctor, not an enabler. The calculated question would linger with him, trouble him, and hopefully, ultimately, release him.

Group

"TIME FOR GROUP," an enthusiastic orderly chirped, poking his head inside Pastor and Max's room.

"Group," the Pastor thought, full of contempt, *"Funny farm would be more apt."* Or *"cuckoo's nest."*

Dr. Hope had cajoled him into sitting through a few of the ward's group therapy sessions. He hated it. Always someone spouting their sob story to a circle of semi-coherent idiots. He had zipped his lip and endured their mind-numbing inanity, and was determined not to attend again.

"Nutbars," he said, directing his scorn at his roommate.

Max returned his look. What did his eyes imply? Sadness? Pity? Compassion?

"What?" the Pastor asked, choosing to take offense.

Max stood up and waited, silent as always.

"I'm not going, Max."

Still, the hobo lingered, unmoved.

Dr. Hope appeared at the door with an expression that screamed, "Agenda!" "Pastor, we've got a new arrival. An enigma. She'll be in group, and if you'll come, I'd like to get your evaluation afterwards."

"What game is she up to?"

"Please," she insisted. "I don't know what to make of her."

Would he take the bait? The show of respect was too much to resist.

"Fine," he grumped, not wanting to seem too enthusiastic. Like that goofball orderly.

He followed her out, Max tagging along.

The Pastor noticed Max had taken to shadowing him, like a guardian or right-hand man. *"Ironic, since he doesn't have one."*

"And everywhere that Mary went, the lamb was sure to go," the Pastor said, needling his new sidekick. Max beamed.

"An enigma" the doctor had said.

"Ya think?" the Pastor thought, repulsed. *"Abomination would suit better."*

The new member of the circle was obviously a man. Or was supposed to be. If cross-dressers could be considered such. And were those breasts?

The Pastor scowled at Dr. Hope, tasting bile in the back of his throat. *"Never again,"* he vowed, *"never again!"*

"I want to introduce our newcomer today," Dr. Hope said, opening the session. "This is her first visit to our group. Her name is Jack. Or do you prefer Jacki? Welcome here."

A few half-hearted claps.

"Actually, it's Jacki (she/her)—I'm in transition."

"I see," Dr. Hope said. "And what would you like to share today?"

"Maybe about how I got here?"

Pastor sighed audibly. *"Here we go,"* he thought with a dour look.

Jacki gathered herself before continuing. "I spent two years growing out my hair. I added cheap extensions for volume and another six inches of length. I bought a gaudy dress and loud pumps at an inner-city thrift store. Next, I browsed YouTube tutorials for hours, learning how *not* to overdo makeup. I broke every rule and, voila! Instant drag queen. But I wasn't trying to disguise myself as a woman."

"No kidding," the Pastor thought. At nearly 6 feet 6 inches and 230 pounds, s/he looked every bit the streetwalking transvestite, right down to the fishnet stockings, sky-blue eyeshadow, heavily painted eye-

brows, and a hint of five o'clock shadow. A few weeks of stubble covered her scalp where her hair had allegedly been.

"And yes, these are real," she said, hoisting a set of double-Ds. "I've been going through some changes, so it wasn't all a disguise."

The Pastor bristled. He felt his face blushing, hot and red. His fists tightened and trembled.

"WHY THE DISGUISE? You should try it sometime. The urge to stare is so strong that people force themselves not to. And for all their training, that includes the TSA folks in the airport. Oh, they flagged me all right, but who really wants to deal with that? Especially when I stink to high heaven of sickly-sweet perfume. And, of course, no obvious weapons—not even an underwire bra. The halter-top and my muffin top belly were the last insult. So, yeah, I was trying for a gag reflex."

"It's working," Pastor thought, barely containing his disgust. *"You are sick!"*

"So, they wave me through with my little handbag—nothing in it but a wallet, passport, makeup kit, and a CD. I was also carrying a battery-charged beard trimmer and a few 'lady-things.' They didn't even make me take off my polyester belt for screening.

"So, I get through security, and the gate is a breeze, except having to wait for boarding. I'm nervous already—starting to sweat—and it's hard not to glare at all the lookie-loos trying to steal glances of the freak. But they never really *see* me, because they have to keep it peripheral.

"And then, just like that, I'm on the plane and buckled into a seat near the back. Until the flight attendants start serving drinks. Then it's *go time.*"

The Pastor had been ready to bolt for the door, but this twist was curious.

"While they're working the snack trolley, I head into the galley restroom and begin with my hair. I had soaked that mass of tangles in absinthe and then let it dry, rinsed it in absinthe again and repeat. Totally flammable! And that's why I'd slathered on the perfume. It didn't really cover the smell. Just made it more pungent. Nothing that would clue anyone in, just a stronger repellent. Or so I hoped.

"Anyway, I pull out the beard trimmer and go to work—shaved it all off in, like, two minutes. Now I've got this giant wad of flammable hair, ready to light. How? With the wooden matches I'd stored under my belt.

"So far, so good, but just to be sure, I pulled the CD from my purse—'Lemonade' by Beyoncé—and cracked it in half. A sharp, broken edge, pointed corner, easy to grip on the round edge with a finger in the half-center hole—the perfect mini-scimitar. Enough to fillet a jugular, if need be."

"Seriously? This freak really is psycho! Sick in the head and violent to boot!"

"So, I finish the quick buzz-cut and stuff the flammable hair in my purse. I slip back into the galley by myself. If anyone comes back there, I can CD them to death, but that's not plan A. Clipped up high on the rear-facing exterior wall of the restroom is an O_2 tank. Not explosive but flammable. I take it down quietly, no witnesses. Imagine the recipe! The matches light up the hair, and the hair ignites the O_2 tank. *Way* better than the exploding underwear!

"And then . . ." A long pause.

"And then, what?" the Pastor demands.

"And then I wake up here! Last I remember, I had removed the oxygen tank and was holding it under my arm. I had bundled ten matches together in my right hand as a mini-torch and the purse full of hair ready in my left. I just needed to open the O_2 tank and then . . . and then I opened my eyes here. In a padded cell.

"Some sky marshal must have made me after all. I don't know how he ambushed me, but I was so caught—red-handed, whatever that means. He takes me down in that tight space, and I'm writhing, and he's shouting over and over, 'Resisting arrest, resisting arrest, resisting arrest,' and then I guess he cold-clocked me. Lights out. Suddenly, I wake up, strapped to a gurney. He probably got a medal for it too! And what'll I get for attempting a terrorist attack on a chock-full jet? Ten years? Twenty? Are they still force-feeding folks like me at Gitmo?"

"You're safe now," Dr. Hope cut in, "No one's taking you to prison." Then she turned to the group. "Jacki is safe," she said to ward off mass hysteria. "You are all safe. She has her own room and no access to anything flammable."

A subtle signal to the orderly, and Jack(i) was whisked away to her "private room."

"MY APOLOGIES, EVERYONE," Dr. Hope said, addressing the half-dozen remaining patients. "I didn't realize Jacki would 'go there.'"

"Well, what did you expect from a tranny terror-ist?" the Pastor said.

Seeing his anger and fear rising in the others, Dr. Hope opted for openness. "Look, the truth is that Jacki isn't a terrorist. She wasn't on an airplane. She didn't try to light a fire. She's just a few weeks off the street. Confused and lost, like we all get, right? I hope we'll work together to help her belong. Belonging is very important to our healing, isn't it?"

Pastor rose abruptly and strode out, Max in tow.

Evaluation

He who busies himself with the sins of others, or judges his brother on suspicion, has not yet even begun to repent or to examine himself so as to discover his own sins.
—St Maximos the Confessor

"WHAT DO YOU THINK, PASTOR?" Dr. Hope asked.

"What do you care?" he replied, still defiant.

"I asked for your evaluation, and I meant it."

The Pastor shifted in his chair. The privacy of her office did nothing to settle him, as if "privacy" means anything in the Ward. Especially with the ever-present Max shadowing him all day long, always watching, always listening. Watching and listening.

"Alright. In my judgment, people like that should be dropped off on an island and left there to rot."

"That's a judgment, alright. But I asked for an evaluation."

He shrugged. "Same difference."

"It's a verdict. Pure condemnation. Jacki doesn't need a judge. She needs a doctor, which means a diagnosis and a prescription."

"He's a bloody abomination. Diagnosis: repugnant. Prognosis: irredeemable." If that seemed cruel, the Pastor was pleased. Hard-nosed judgment was exactly what he was hoping to communicate.

Max became agitated.

"Max," Dr. Hope said, "it might be best if Pastor and I had some alone time." Max refused to budge. Hope thought twice and decided against calling for the orderly.

"Is that how you would preach?" she asked.

"Absolutely."

"And people responded to cruelty?"

"Cruelty? It's not cruelty. They respond to the truth. They respond to holiness, and to divine justice."

"To brow-beating?"

"No, it's not brow-beating. Think of it as…as a form of penance."

"How so?"

"They come in dirty hedonists, get their whippin', and leave feeling clean."

"Or bruised."

"If so, they thanked me for it."

"So, 'I *do* condemn you. Go and sin no more.'"

"Now you're getting it. It's an act of righteous mercy."

"And what about broken people? People on the edge? People like Jacki."

"We didn't attract many folks like him."

"Your turn-or-burn message wouldn't help much, would it?"

"It helps them move right along."

"For a pastor, that seems pretty cold."

"I'm not there to make them feel comfortable with being hell bound. The broad road leads to destruction. Ours is a narrow gate, and few find it. Few are meant to find it."

"Well, at least you're not bitter," Dr. Hope replied. The humor didn't translate. Max's head hung low.

The Pastor wasn't sure whether he felt a twinge of conscience or morbid curiosity, but felt led to ask, "Jack didn't try to firebomb a jet?"

"No. As I said, she's just off the street."

"And not a tranny either?"

"You mean transvestite? Transgender? Transsexual?"

"Yeah, whatever. It doesn't matter."

"It matters to *her*."

"*Him.*"

"I thought it didn't matter."

The Pastor's nostrils flared in annoyance. "Do you want my evaluation or not? What's *his* story anyway?"

Dr. Hope knew she was cornered. She couldn't break doctor-client confidentiality, and this was about observing the Pastor's reaction, not sharing Jacki's backstory.

"Look," she explained, "I told the group that Jacki poses no threat to any of you. What does that tell you?"

"That he's a chronic liar. Or delusional. Or has stupid nightmares."

"Could be any of those. So, why would she wake up here?"

"An overdose?"

"Or?"

"Someone knocked her on the head?"

"Or?"

"Some kinda stroke."

"So, which of those possibilities do you deem 'irredeemable?'"

"Well, he's still a tranny—whatever type. That's just sick."

"What sickness might that be? Seriously, play it out."

The Pastor stopped and thought. "He's one thing inside and pretending to be another on the outside. He's a man pretending to be a woman—or trying to convince himself that he is a woman."

"Or a woman who woke up with male parts, trying to become herself."

"Agree to disagree on that one, doc."

"Fair enough. In either case, we can agree that she is deeply conflicted. And the airplane story tells us that something broke. And now she is here. Shall we leave her to it or apply some compassionate care?"

"Not my problem."

"That's true. You are not required to fix her, heal her, judge her, or condemn her. You are completely off the hook, but thanks for your evaluation."

The Pastor shrugged. "Don't mention it."

The Doctor stopped collecting papers and looked up, "Would you tell me something, does it feel good?"

"Does what feel good?"

"Not being responsible for anyone's journey but your own."

"Sure. Feels great," he said flippantly. "Light, actually."

Now she paused, laying aside her work and looked at him intently. "Pastoring must have been heavy. Carrying the burden for other's souls. The obligation to save all those people. It must have been exhausting."

"I guess," he offered suspiciously even while sensing a huge weight.

"Must feel good to just let it go."

The Pastor felt conflicted. Really? Could he let just let it go? Even pondering that hypothetically felt like a ton of cinder blocks might slip off his knotted shoulders. But it also felt threatening. Foreboding. Why was that? What was this dread? *"If I were to let go . . ."*

"So, is 'Pastor' who you are or who you pretend to be?"

"Huh?" It took him a second to refocus.

"Is there actually a pastor *in there*," the doctor tapped her heart, "or is someone inside suffering from wearing the heavy pastor persona for too long?"

The Pastor brooded, no quick diverting retort coming to his rescue.

Dr. Hope rephrased the question. "Jacki is trying to become a woman. We know this. But on the inside, we can't agree if Jacki is a he or a she. We just know that something broke, and here she is.

"But what about you? We know you were trying to be a good pastor. Yet here you are. Something broke. So, on the inside, who will I find? A pastor who's exhausted and wants to be someone else, or someone else who's been trying to be the Pastor? And if so, why?"

The Pastor couldn't answer. Wouldn't answer. The brief window of clarity was shuttered again, and he suddenly felt his right hand was not where he thought it should be.

When had Max taken hold of it?

the Visitor

"PASTOR, YOU HAVE A VISITOR," the orderly said.

The Pastor jerked upright from the common room puzzle and beat a hasty path to the toilet. Barely made it. Well, almost made it. Anxiety-attacks activate human fight-or-flight systems, triggering an uncontrollable adrenaline rush that redistributes water and blood flow. Endgame: sudden-onset diarrhea.

Something is wrong. I'm not supposed to have visitors. Doctor's orders. My orders.

"Are you alright?" the orderly asked through the door.

"Gimme a minute." The Pastor waited out the convulsions, then cleaned up as best he could. He tried to slow his breathing. He realized he was panting and damp everywhere with a cold sweat. He washed a second time and dragged his fingers through his hair.

I can do this. But who . . . ?

When he came out, ever faithful Max was there, waiting with the orderly. His head was cocked to the side, inquisitive, and he looked concerned.

"Look out, I gotta change," the Pastor said, brushing between them and heading to his room for some fresh clothes. "Where's Dr. Hope?"

"Not in today," the orderly replied, following him patiently.

"I'm not receiving visitors yet."

"Well, somehow she was on the list. Take your time, Pastor. But I think you're going to want to see her," he said with a wink.

It makes no sense, but if the wife has really come . . . Yes, okay, I can do this."

THERE SHE WAS. Pixie haircut, black power suit, dark eyes—dark like daggers. *Not* his faithful wife.

"Shit!" And he nearly did. The last face he'd seen before his meltdown. The Mona Lisa smirk—but more accusatory than coy.

"Well, hello, Pastor," the Visitor said with cynical cheer. "Remember me?" Her voice was a cold knife sliding between his ribs.

At those two words, memories flooded his mind. Shameful and shaming images clawing at him . . . strangling him.

The Pastor reeled, fought for consciousness, grabbed at the railing that lined the facility walls.

For the second time, this Visitor's—this Adversary's—unexpected presence ignited images that coagulated into an onrush of memories. Like demons escaping from hell, apparitions from the past pried their way out of the closet he had so sealed shut through force of will—when his nervous system was stronger. But relentless stress, repeated crises, and plain old aging had weakened the door of denial. His defenses, now feeble, splintered open. He overheard guttural sounds moaning from within, like prisoners organizing a revolt. It was an onslaught.

Some say hitting rock bottom is when we finally surrender. But it never begins there. We have to break through denial—a hellish and involuntary experience that epitomizes the loss of control. Never at the time or place of our choosing. Rock bottom begins when every coping mechanism finally breaks under the weight of our secrets and the lies we tell ourselves to keep them hidden.

The Pastor's cataclysmic collapse was particularly acute, because, for whatever reason, his psyche could never completely segregate the various ghastly episodes of his roughly six decades. Every trauma, every shameful act, every wound was stuffed into one big vault. Well, not big enough, apparently.

For years he had released the internal pressure through the valve of hellfire preaching, but the gauge had red-lined and finally blown when the Visitor appeared out of nowhere. And here she was, again. That's when the dam of memories completely burst in an explosive flood of darkness. Not only the godawful flashbacks of this demon's hold on him . . . other memories, older secrets, filthier deeds . . . sounds, smells, disgusting painful sensations . . . of being held down, violated, ripped apart.

That's when he threw up, and things went black. He was flailing again, thrashing in the dark. "*You filthy bastards! I'll kill ya! I'll kill ya all!*"

A miracle! His hands had groped their way around her scrawny throat, and the two of them fell to the ground together. He was on top of her, willing himself not to look at her, blindly squeezing. The orderly was shouting, the sound of running feet, hands forcefully trying to pull him away, but he would not let go. He had her . . . had *them all*. Every single one of them, from all those times.

"Stop! Pastor, stop! Somebody stop him!" someone screamed.

But this time the adrenaline did not fail him.

Rather than go to his bowels, the strength of seven men went to his fists—vices of justice, retribution, revenge. "*If Cain is avenged seven times, then Lamech seventy-seven times!*"

And then he felt it, an exhilarating crunch as he crushed her trachea and twisted it violently. He could feel the gush of warm blood pouring over his hands from her mouth. A final gurgle punctuated the fatal eruption. It was finished.

"Let me through! I've got him!" Powerful arms enfolded him from behind, squeezing his arms tight to his body. The large hands pried loose his bloody fingers. "Pastor! Pastor, let him go! I've got you. Please, stop!"

He didn't even feel the first syringe as an orderly jabbed him with a sedative.

"Hit him again!" someone yelled. Another pinprick. Then another. Dizziness overtook him. He was ready anyway. He was done. He had won.

A split second before passing out, The Pastor opened his eyes.

He was lying there, straightjacketed by Jacki's arms.

The Visitor wasn't there.

Next to him on the floor was Max.

Broken and lifeless.

"No! Jesus . . ." the Pastor groaned, then slipped mercifully into unconsciousness.

THE CELL

a Meditation

I felt for the tormented whirlwinds
damned for their carnal sins
committed when they let their passions
rule their reason.
—Dante's Inferno

ONCE BITTEN, TWICE SHY.

When self-will—the delusion of autonomy—leads inexorably to rock bottom, its mirror opposite is the paralysis of resignation, where you simply don't care anymore.

Resignation is not surrender, but just a lateral step away.

Hold your hands in front of you, palms down, and allow one wrist to fall completely limp (like Adam in Michelangelo's, "The Creation of Adam"). Let the limp hand represent lethargy, listlessness, defeat—resignation.

We may refuse to participate in life, expecting some other to act on us independently. "Just fix me!" we say from our cave or beneath our covers.

And when our spouse's care, our therapist's answers, our pharmacist's remedies, or our God's mighty hand fail to save as we had hoped or demanded, we may retreat to the sidelines as depressed observers or jeering cynics.

There are words and wounds tatooed on this lethargic hand. Read them: fatigue, relinquishment, despair, hopelessness. Nor will a last gasp of self-will save us—that was the serpent in Eden that bit us from the beginning. Our best efforts expelled us from Paradise. We cannot be saved by that which poisoned us.

Where the clenched fist said, "If God won't do it, *I will*," the limp wrist abdicates: "If God won't do it, *why should I?*"

Many a spiritual leader masquerades as "contemplative" but is reduced to numbing out the needs of others, hiding from their darkness in the deeper darkness of their secret addictions. Untreated, burnout leads to blow-up, and with it, the collateral damage of spiritual abuse. Self-will controls, self-pity seduces. Who's to say which creates more casualties?

From burnout to blow-up to bottom-out.

From the sidelines to the shelf.

Or the cell.

THE PASTOR FOUND HIMSELF in restraints, but both hands hung limp—his body all but lifeless.

It was that moment when one emerges from a nightmare only to realize the waking hell is worse than the night terrors. The panic attack was already kicking in before he was fully awake. The Pastor craned his neck around, saw the bare walls, the metal door with its small window, the tall ceiling, and the surveillance camera up in the corner.

He remembered.

The Visitor. The assault.

His hands, crushing her throat.

But, it was Max's throat.

Oh, Max. Dead—murdered. By him.

He remembered. Remembered Jacki's massive arms constraining him.

Jacki begging him to let go.

Would he ever be able to?

Let go? After what he'd done?

With even a hint of awareness came a wave of panic. Without mercy it slammed into his heart and lungs. Hyperventilation.

The door clanged open. An orderly. Another orderly. Another sedative. Thank you!

Asleep again. The nightmare. The waking hell. Panic. Sedative. Sleep.

The cycle continued through days. Weeks?

At last, he awoke, not in panic but numb and re-signed.

The panic had said, "This cannot be. This must not be."

Resignation said, "This is" and "I'm in hell."

"No, you're not."

Who was that?
A voice?

"Who's there?"

No one.
Just a voice.

"Or maybe you are. In hell, yes, maybe you are."

"Who . . . ?"

"Specifically, you're in lock-up. Solitary. The bug-ward. The golden gown gives you away. That's so if you escape, the cops will know you're wacko. But don't worry, you won't escape. Ever."

"Who . . . who are you?"

"It's not really gold though—the gown. It's baby-shit mustard."

"What the . . . who?"
Wait, the voice.
That Voice.

"Shit, just like you!" she shouted.

The Voice became a face. *Her* face. Hovering inches above his.
The Visitor!
"How . . . ?"
He writhed frantically in the padded straps on his wrists and ankles.
His face crawled in a fire-red blush.
Panic. Couldn't breathe.

"Ah, still not at bottom, hmm?"
With a demonic cackle, she disappeared.

Panic. The cycle resumed.
The door, the orderly, the sedative, the nightmare.
Waking hell. And another visit from his tormenter.
The monitors could not hear her. But he could.
The camera did not see her. But he did.

She sat on the end of his bed, scowling at him, deriding him.

She stood over him, breathing heavily into his face.

Reminding him. Shaming him. Accusing him.

"You don't even remember my name, do you... Pastor?"

"I . . . uh . . ."

"Our little secret, hmm?"

(His words, long ago).

She ran an icy hand up his leg, under his gown

(as he once did).

"No, don't . . . please, don't," he winced

(as she once did).

But she did. Probing where she ought not

(as he once had).

"Am I turning you on?" she asked

(as he once had).

"No . . . no, you're hurting me," he whimpered

(as she once did).

"You told yourself I'd forget. But I never forgot. I remember. You told yourself *you* would forget. But you remember," she seethed sadistically, inflicted more pain until he groaned

(as she once had).

"You didn't just remember, did you, Pastor? You clung to it, didn't you? To our little secret."

"I . . . I was ashamed." Tears streaked down his cheeks into his ears.

"You clung to the shame." Hurting him again.

"Yes . . ."

"No! Not just the shame. Clung to the power."

"No . . ." He wheezed miserably as she became more violent.

"Yes! Clung to your precious power. How is it you're still lying, even now?"

She pulled off her belt, climbed onto him, straddled his chest.

"What . . . what are you doing?" he asked. "I'm sorry! I'm sorry!"

"Sorry? You're not sorry, you idiot. You're terrified. You think I came for an apology? No, this is about justice, punishment . . . *this is vengeance!*"

She wrapped the leather strap around his neck, twisted it tight, choking him. "Welcome to my lie detector! Tell me, Pastor, our powerful little secret. Did you replay it? Not for shame but to relive the power?"

"N-n-n-ooo," he squeaked.

"*Liar.* Yes or no: violating me was a fantasy you imagined again and again in your sick mind."

"Noooo," he gasped.

"*Liar*." She tightened the belt even more, leaning into his ear. "You replayed it in your mind even when you made love to your wife! *Didn't you?*"
She released the knot, and he caught a quick breath. He tried to cry out, but she jammed the belt into his mouth, to the back of his throat, making him gag (as she once had).

Then she bit him hard, left deep marks in his left shoulder (as he had done), breaking his skin, bloodying him. Bit him again. And again.

No more—he could take it no more. There was no point. He went limp.

She pulled the belt from his mouth.

"Yes!" he cried. "Yes, it's true. But . . . but it was so long ago."

"So long ago! Yet you remember. And you remembered and remembered and remembered again. Did you imagine I wouldn't?" She lashed him with words and the belt, leaving welts up and down his body.

"You don't remember my name."

"I . . . I do. Your name . . . you're . . . Mallory."

"Yes, Mallory. But no. That foster brat is long gone. Probably overdosed in an alley somewhere. You did that! You drove her there! And your wife knew about it, didn't she? Who does that to a child? And to how many others? In the name of 'care'? Used her up till she ran away. But you didn't know she'd find a home inside your head—and that *I would be there with her*, did you?"

"Mallory?"

She slapped him across the face. "Not Mallory. What's my name? I'll tell you."

And then he heard her name, loudly in his mind rather than his ears.

I am Shame.
I am Adversary.
I am your Accuser.

"Then his lord said unto him," she said pompously, "'O thou wicked servant.' And his lord was wroth, and delivered him to the tormentors, till he should pay all that was due unto him."

She reached back and did something to him. Knife-like. Mutilating.

"Jesus! Jesus!" he screamed. "Help! Help me!"

She disappeared, vaporized in a snap.

The orderlies rushed in the door for the umpteenth time, but this time the Pastor was already out.

Assessment

THE PASTOR WAS LUCID, but he couldn't wake himself up.

He could hear everything. He could hear her voice. He could even see her, whether with his mind's eye or his vacant material eyes, he did not know.

Not the Visitor. It was Dr. Hope.

"He's catatonic. Like when he first arrived."

"What happened?" a second voice asked.

"Another panic attack but more severe. It led to a seizure. And odd phenomena."

"Phenomena?"

"Marks on his body. Not ones he gave himself."

"How? Who?"

"The camera recordings are complete. No one came in or left this cell. But the patient appeared to have a grand mal, then raised welts appeared on his body—his thighs, arms, even his chest. And this appeared spontaneously on camera." She pointed to his neck—bruising and abrasions all the way around.

"Psychosomatic?"

"Hard to say, but look. Do these seem self-in-flicted to you?" She teased back the gauze. Three deep human bite marks scarred the Pastor's shoulders.

"Whoa. Uh, well, Doctor, before we call in Stephen King for a consult, let's allow for the wonders and enigmas of the human psyche. The forces of the subconscious account for more than we know."

Dr. Hope raised an eyebrow. "Agreed. And would the 'forces of the subconscious' account for this?" She pulled up the front of the Pastor's gown.

"Oh gawd!" her associate groaned. "Can that be . . . repaired?"

"With extensive plastic surgery, maybe. Better question: after this, can *he* be repaired?"

"And the catatonia?"

"I have a hypothesis—a hope. Some trauma seems impossible to work out even with decades of therapy. But I've witnessed a few cases where dementia over-takes the consciousness—and in a long-term catatonic state, the subconscious mind processes issues we could never reach. Healing comes, and not just through the passage of time. Somehow, the patients are working out internally what they can't face here."

"How would you verify that?"

"In the cases I've seen, they wake up at peace. Similar perhaps to near-death experiences. But the point is, their madness compels them past their waking denial and into their psychotic darkness. Yet somehow, they aren't abandoned there. They find their way out."

"So, they go to sleep broken and wake up whole?"

"No, I don't think they just go to sleep. I suspect they go through 'hell.' But that's the thing: some go through it . . . and come back."

"They recover?"

"Mmmm . . . they would lapse back into a coma or die shortly thereafter. But the important thing is that something ugly—their torment—died *before* they came back. It's like they made their peace with God."

"Or with themselves—I'm not the religious type. But let's say you're right. How long, typically?"

"I don't see it often, but the cases I witnessed spanned a decade."

"Well, I suppose that might count as time served."

Memories

Exile is possible within the beauty of the infinite only by way of an exilic interiority, a fictive inwardness, where the creature can grasp itself as an isolated essence. ...Absolute subjective liberty is only known in hell, where the fire of divine beauty is held at bay.

Hell is the purest interiority, a palpable fiction, a turning in, a fabrication of an inward depth, a shadow, a privation, a loss of the whole outer world, a refusal of the surface.

It makes no difference here whether one speaks of death, sin or hell: in each case one speaks of the same privation, the same estranging history, the same limit shattered at Easter.

—David Bentley Hart, *The Beauty of the Infinite*

MEMORIES ARE SHADOWS—tricky business. Subjective and suggestible, reconstructive and malleable. The events of our lives are done and gone, but memories persist as animated, impressionist art—and as storehouses of our joy and sorrow. Are they real? The patient's sorrow, anger, and fear were real—and so he saw what he saw, all too vividly.

THE BOY WAS IN A LOCKER ROOM, alone. The other boys were in the next room, dressing for practice. They had shoved him hard and locked him out, leaving him to change alone.

But the trio of bullies came in. They shouted profanities, shaming him with labels he would wear for years. He kept his head down and began to shake uncontrollably.

"Don't piss yourself," he said, hiding inside his mind. *"Just don't piss yourself. And don't cry. For God's sake, don't let them see you cry."*

The mocking was relentless, loud, and hurtful, tattooing his soul, emasculating him.

Now they were not just throwing words—they were throwing stuff. He could duck that alright. But not the spit—there was no eluding the downpour of thick greenish sludge.

He couldn't take it. The boy screamed. Every

swear word he knew. He grabbed his duffle bag and swung it around and around, buying precious space from them before they could commence with the pummeling.

Of course, the coach would have to show up just then. There was finger-pointing and lies and false witnesses, and the coach witnessed his guilt firsthand. So, it was all on him. *All* on him. All *in* him.

This he would *not* forgive. This would come out. One day.

Violently.

THEY STUFFED THE BOY IN A LOCKER. Two of them—yes, two other bullies, another place, another year—forced him into a small hallway locker. They had no idea of his claustrophobia, but anyone would have felt the squeeze in there.

At first, he fought, but they delivered discreet body blows, so no one would see. *Of course, they saw,* but they remained silent. Better him than them.

The boy finally succumbed, let them jam him into the enclosed space. He thought he'd go mad with panic, but he didn't. He was safe from them now. And so, he learned to hide in lockers—as a joke—and they let him. Stupid kid. Problem solved.

Or was it?

I was caught in a cauldron of hate.
I felt persecuted and paralyzed.

THE BOY WAS IN A DORM, sprawled out on a bed, twisting violently, kicking.

"Hold him!" one of the boys yelled.

Two others were laughing, grasping at his thrashing limbs. A different trio—another place and time. The instigator stood above his head, out of view, clamped down on his wrists, and pulled his arms above and behind his head. The other two each wrestled a leg. Boy #2 held his right shin in a bear hug. But the boy managed to wrench his left foot free, flailing it wildly. He clocked Boy #3 with a boot to the side of the head, and their laughter turned to anger and aggression. The boy was puzzled that they should be offended by his retaliation—they almost made him feel guilty.

Finally, he was pinned down.

"Pull down his pants," the alpha male said.

"Yeah," his cohorts jeered, complying with relish. "His shorts too!"

Down came his shorts, leaving him naked and ashamed, a victim of their mockery of his anatomy.

He tried to jerk away again, but they pressed heavily on him.

"Use that," Alpha said.

Boy #2 brandished some unseen object.

The boy clenched his buttocks with all his might.

It was so weird how the next day, everyone—including him—acted as if nothing had changed. Same dorm life, same pecking order—living together, eating together, playing together. None of the boys, not even he, thought of it as sexual assault. It was just a dorm prank, "good-natured" hazing. And they weren't gay or anything. The boy forgave them and moved on.

NO. No, he didn't. He swallowed the bitter pill—stored it for future use. And abuse.

REALLY YOUNG. The boy could never understand what he had done to be so hated. Maybe he had said something he shouldn't. Sometimes he was clumsy and broke something. But often he was just quietly eating supper or doodling with crayons when his father's face darkened, and his glare turned on the boy. For no reason, it seemed. But to the boy, there had to be a reason. He would only be despised if he was despicable, right? Treated like dirt if he really was dirt, right?

"You piece of dirt!" his father shouted. In the shed, the boy would be strapped to a bench, his father towering over him. Then the belt would come. The first time, the pain of the whipping was excruciating, and he couldn't hold back his high-pitched screams. Only the first time. After that, he managed to dissociate and would watch the beating from somewhere in the rafters. Detached from the scene, he could hear the boy's cries, but it wasn't him. It wasn't him.

NOT YET FIVE YEARS OLD. "I oughta kill you, Diaper." Why did he call the boy diaper? Because he was full of shit. That was the message. Unwisely, he had spoken one night, and now the man held him by the throat, suspended over the dark water at the end of their dock. And he believed it. This was the end.

But it wasn't the end. His father pulled him up and dragged him back to the shed. After his beating, he padlocked him in overnight.

The boy went fetal and shook with little tremors throughout the night—literally in shock. He should have died. No, he really should have.

BAD MEMORIES. But he had taken it, right? Dealt with it, hadn't he? In his own way. Buried them. Sort of. But what's that proverb about burying the dead cat, only to dig it up again later, rottener and smellier than before? True enough.

But when it came to the other children in his family, he could *not* take it. The boy was super-sensitive, hyper-empathetic. What about them? The brothers and sisters and cousins he couldn't protect or fix. The boy carried more worry than any child could bear.

Caught in a double-bind between powerlessness and vengeance, when others—family members, uncles, cousins (victims and offenders)—began to die of self-harm, he vowed he'd fix it. Promised himself. Promised God.

These vows born in bitterness, this calling rooted in repressed rage, formed the boy into the Pastor—the contradiction of abuse and fundamentalism. (No, that's not a contradiction.)

"Engulfed in a fever of spite," the boy became the beast he meant to slay.

Is there no good thing in me?

Dreams

WITH THE MEMORIES came recurring dreams.
Or dreams of memories.
Symbolic or surreal, all were true.
Or my truth in this unstable Netherworld.

THE SOJOURN

I am a child, just four or five, lost and alone,
hiding in a barn.

I am a long way from home.
My clothes are dripping, my eyes sag heavily.
The fog is all encompassing,
filling my surroundings with white.
I am all alone in a barn.
I sit on the hay floor facing the threshold
of rainfall only a foot away.

The percussion on the tin roof allows me to stop
thinking about my breathing for a moment

I refuse to sleep in my bed
I roll over into the nest of clothing
scattered over the ground.
Each piece carries a familiar scent
and excites my skin with a new texture.

I am overcome with homesickness.
I don't know
whether I should keep my eyes open or not.
Dusk comes and goes
before I have a chance to notice,
preoccupying myself with memories,
slipping into dreams.

The insides of my eyelids are red
from the light of day.
I orient myself
with the sounds of wind in the grass,
on my skin, and in my lungs.
I open my eyes.

RECURRING DREAM

I dream that I die, and I dream it again. And
again.
I die but the dream continues.
But it wasn't really an afterlife.
I would just die, and then "nothing" would happen. There wasn't black or white or consciousness—just fear and the feeling of a frail husk
crumbling in on itself.
Eventually, I would fade into sleep again, and I'd
wake up unnerved.

THE VINE

Months pass, as best I can tell.
I have a vision of being the husk again,
now close to dust.
But a vine starts growing from the dust and flakes.
The vine sprouts with flowers as it grew,
and once it encompasses all of me,
it grows outward,
reaching out.

Sage

"IN THE END, IT WAS ALL ABOUT FEAR. Fear stopped you from walking in the sunlight of the Spirit."

A voice. A visitor.

"Oh God, please not her. Not Mallory."

No, not *her*. Another.

The Pastor peeked out from his stasis. He was sitting up. The restraints had been removed ages ago—unnecessary after the seizures subsided. He didn't, *couldn't,* move a muscle—not on his own anyway—apart from automatonic chewing, swallowing, or shuffling to the loo or shower, and only with help of aides. So, to avoid bedsores, they regularly sat him up in a medically fitted chair.

He was still in lockdown—a private room with minimal amenities. No television, no window—no glass. Protective custody, so to speak. Just a few bright paintings and, occasionally, piped-in music. Not that

he heard it. Catatonics don't experience time or awareness like we do. Their brains are not dead, but they do
hibernate—like a laptop in sleep mode.

Then, like when someone touches the keyboard,
a dream may come, or a nurse's voice may stimulate
glimmers of recognition—nothing more.

"Knock, knock," she said.

"Who's there?"

"Ah, awake, are we?

"You can hear me?"

"Of course, I can hear you. My name is Sage."

"Sage?" a lump formed in his throat, another in
his gut. Would he soil himself?

"Yes, that Sage. You remember, don't you? I do.
Every detail, every time, believe me. But don't be
afraid; I'm not going hurt you. Your fear—that's why
I'm here."

"You won't hurt me? You're not here to punish me?"

She pulled up the one chair in the room and took
his limp hand in hers.

"Seems like you've been punished plenty. What
did that solve? Sure, it broke you. I guess that's something. But has it healed you? Has it healed Mallory?"

The Pastor's eyes glistened with sadness.

"No, Pastor. Perversion carries its own price—like
this paralyzing fear that's locked you inside."

(As he had done to her.)

"And yet it still has its way with you."

(As he had with her.)

"The fear you put in me—*the fear of God* you called it—well, it did a number on me. Nearly killed me. Tempted me to kill you. But no amount of harm or self-harm I could muster, either as medication or as punishment, ever cured me of the fear. It's that fear that's killing you."

"Fear won't ever leave me."

"I don't know that it will. But I can say this: it left me. Completely. I'm not afraid anymore—not even of you. I'm free."

"How?"

"I used to think my fear was that I didn't try hard enough or wasn't being good enough. That if I could just get it right, the abuse would stop. But I couldn't, and I didn't."

"I did that to you."

"Yes, you put that there. And as the good Lord said, 'Anyone who puts a cause for stumbling in one of these little ones, it would be better for him to have a millstone hung around his neck and be thrown into the sea.'"

"Yes. It would be."

"But that wasn't the deepest fear. My fear was that I—myself, Sage—was not worthy of love. And that has been your fear, all your life, hasn't it?"

"But it's true. I'm not. Not at all worthy of love. Look at me. What I've done. Who I am."

"That is the fear on which you built your pulpit, your ministry of condemnation—so deeply rooted in shame—in order to separate yourself from humanity. You alienated others, exploited them, and they reacted. You used their resentments to justify your own self-hatred, and spewed it on everyone in the name of 'God.'"

"Yes, I see it. I did that."

The awful truth. Bitter but effective.

"And what if you were to let go?"

"Let go?"

"What if you were to let go of the fear that you are not worthy of love? Why continue punishing yourself for your sins and being slaughtered by the reactions of others, reactions that you perpetrated? Why do you continue to let fear own you? Why give two shits? Instead of 'F-off' or 'Let me explain,' how about just 'Bye-bye'? Let it go."

"Let it go? How can I—?"

"Look, *your* heroics got you here. All these struggles—what's the common denominator? You—your fear. And your fear has incapacitated you. So, it's not about 'How can I?'"

"What then? Faith?"

"Oh, you have lots of faith. Trouble was, you left out God—left out Love and Grace. Your only part now is to surrender . . . and then you wait."

"But I did surrender. Look at me."

"No, you gave up—you resigned, because playing god kicked your ass. Now it's time for you to surrender *to* Grace. You're a pastor. Do you understand nothing about Grace? Don't you know you're already forgiven?"

"I've never been good at grace."

"Ya think?"

"In my head, but I don't feel it."

"Oh, I hadn't noticed," she said sarcastically, but it didn't feel mean. "Trust me, been there. Why don't you feel forgiveness? Because you don't know Grace. Because you still haven't resigned as your own judge. When you let go of the gavel and start forgiving yourself . . ."

"I can't. I want to. But I don't know how."

"It always seems to come down to this: what if you're not the piece of shit you think you are? That was Shame talking—the Adversary, the Accuser. Grace says, 'While you were still Love's enemy, She forgave you.' And 'deserve' has nothing to do with it. That's the spiritual surrender your little religious bean can't fathom. You just don't get it, do ya?"

"No, I don't. When I remember . . ."

The Pastor stumbled, obsessing over his unveiled sins and sickness. His fractured mind was stuck and losing the plot.

"Okay, then," Sage said, "remember what you've already been through, breaking through denial—it's like giving birth to your own head—and how painful that was. And remember when you had to let go of the idea that you knew what the hell to do, how you saw all that you had been building was a fantasy and how it all blew up and destroyed those girls. And now a man is dead—a good and kind man. An innocent man."

"You're hurting me. Killing me."

"No, the truth is hurting you and you have been killing yourself. But don't be afraid; you're not dying. You're in labor. I'm just the midwife. And this is where you cooperate with the contractions and push—where you decide: Love is, or Love is not. The Light is or there is no Light. I am in or I am out. I will keep living, or I will keep dying. And when you surrender— because you will—the doors will fly open."

"But why? What?"

"With this surrender, it's not about the whys but the how and the what."

"*What do I do?*"

"You let go."

"*How?*"

"Will you pray something with me?"

"*Anything, anything. Please ...*"

"Okay, pray this: 'Hey Love!'"

"*Dear God . . . er, Love . . .*"

"I know you're busy in Beirut,"

"*What?*"

"Trust me. Just pray it."

"*I know you're busy . . .*"

"But Buddy, I could use some help here."

"*Help me.*"

"Excuse me, Love ..."

"*Excuse me, God ...*"

"But what the hell?"

"*What?*"

"Not religious enough for you, Pastor? Because your grandiose soliloquies have worked so well? When will you finally get real and honest with the Big Guy?"

"*I'm sorry. I'm trying. I'm really trying. Please, don't give up on me.*"

"Okay, I'll make it simple." Step by step, she led him to pray.

I'm powerless, but you are able.

Remove this fear from me, and show me how to live.

Forgive me, and help me forgive myself.

He waited.

"I don't feel anything."

"Really? Shucks, I guess the spell didn't work."

"What?"

"This isn't magic. Newsflash: Love isn't your genie, jumping when you snap your fingers. This is daily surrender and waiting for Grace to do what Love wills when they will it."

"How long?"

"Why? Somewhere you gotta be?" Sage laughed. "Actually, that's a decent prayer. 'How long, O Lord?' Yes, maybe you're getting the hang of this.

"Look, Pastor, if you were a well, you've spent decades muddying the water, filling yourself with filth and silt. What's the mud? Fear, resentment, anger, ingratitude. What removes the dirt? Grace, of course. Only Grace. You don't heal yourself, but at the same time, Grace doesn't heal you instantly or magically. It's Love's process, but you participate."

"But you said it was all Grace."

"Honey, you don't make the pie—not one crumb. But you do have to eat it, every last crumb. But we don't like that, do we? 'Just zap me, God!' Sorry, but it doesn't work that way. Or haven't you noticed?"

"Then how does it work? Please, what's my part?"

"Your part? Stick with your Grace routine, and watch for Love."

"Grace routine? What's my Grace routine?"

"Let's make it easy, so you don't mess it up. Ready? Wake up, pee, listen to Grace, surrender. Then wait for Love. Got it?"

"I don't know. I'm a terrible listener."

"True. But rumor has it you've been hearing voices. The voice of Shame, the voice of the Adversary, the voice of Hope, even the voice of Wisdom—that's me, by the way. Maybe one of these days, the voice you hear will be Love. That voice—the kind voice—that's Grace."

"Grace or Love?"

"Yes. Or Spirit and Truth. Whatever. They're One—in cahoots."

"I don't know Grace. I wouldn't know true Love if it I saw it."

"No, you don't. But you will. What is Grace? When things are shit, and you get through it. When the worst happens, and it becomes the best thing. That's Grace."

"It's hard."

"Yes, but not rock hard. It's ice hard. Surrender, and this too shall melt."

"Why does it have to be so hard?"

"Where would we be without turmoil? Without the fight? The truth is, we've never been without the Light of Grace, but this wretched journey is waking you up, opening your eyes to it. You know what? You've never been closer to it. But as a wise fish once said, 'Just keep swimming, just keep swimming . . .'"

Forgiveness

SAGE, FAITHFUL SAGE. Another visit from the one he once ruined—*despoiled*. After what he'd done, why would she come? Why help him?

"What have you heard?"

"Heard"? The Pastor knew she was referring to his "Grace routine."

"Same thing every day. 'Be still and know that I am Love. Be still and know. Be still. Be.' That's it."

"That's great, Pastor! See? You can do this."

"Do what? What good does it do? I'm already still. Can't move so much as an eyelid."

"You blink."

"Not on purpose."

"Excellent. 'How to Be – preschool 101.'"

"Not funny."

"Pretty funny. But also true. Every moment of stillness is *unto* something."

"Unto what?"

"Well, unto not freaking out, for one. No panic attacks in how long?"

"Also, not funny. Time means nothing here."

"But a long time, right?"

"And anyway, I'm catatonic."

"Sure, but inside, the fear is draining, bit by bit."

"I guess".

"And the peace?"

"A little. Some days. Moments."

"Be grateful. But the stillness has been prepping you."

"For what?"

Fear. Instantly. So much for moments.

"Shhh. For forgiveness."

"No change on that front."

"We'll see. Me and Grace, we were talking, see?"

"Really? And?"

"He wants to show you something. Could be hard, but remember: only ice hard."

"Something I did"? he asked, trembling inside.

"Yes. But something you've already been forgiven for. He just wants you to know."

"I . . . I don't know. I'm afraid."

"Yes. But you're also ready. He told me so. And he has never lied to me yet."

"I'm ready?"

"I promise."

A long silence.

"Take your time. Just sayin'." Her smile was warm. Encouraging. Which was also distressing. In his life of conniving and control and brokenness—the harms he'd done, even to her—the Pastor had become hyper vigilant. Even in her kindness, or because of it, he half-expected Sage to turn on him, finishing the job Mallory had begun.

It may have been a minute or many hours. He waited. Still she stayed. He fought for stillness. And she stayed. *"Just be,"* he thought, then finally surrendered.

"Ready?" she asked.

"I thought you said I was!"

"So, I did. And so, did you know who." She pointed up.

Yes, "I'm ready," the Pastor said humbly. His bravado had died what seemed a lifetime ago—another victory of Grace.

HE SAW A THRONE and someone sitting on it. No, it was a cross. *The* Cross, in fact. And someone hanging from it—a King, wearing a crown. No, thorns. But in his vision, it was all one and the same.

And he heard the Voice, from the Cross.

"Tell *me* what you did."

"I did this. We all did."

The Pastor knew this—in his head, theologically.

"Tell me *what* you did."

"I did this. I participated. What I did to them, I did to you."

Now he saw it—with his eyes. The gore of a crucifixion. The nudity. The violation. The head games and power tripping. And what it did to them, to *Him*.

"Tell me what *you* did."

"I know I did this."

And then he saw. Truly saw for the first time. Saw and *felt*—without escaping through denial, without the self-centeredness of shame, without the terror of being caught, without the self-pity of consequences, without the narcissism of self-loathing. At last he truly *felt* what *they* endured with purified empathy. What *they* felt—not how what they felt made *him* feel.

"Tell me what you *did*."

STRIPPED OF EVERY DEFENSE (and every fear), the Pastor remembered exactly and confessed explicitly before Grace and in the presence of another human being the exact nature of his wrongs.

It took eight hours, if time meant anything there.

All of it. He left out nothing. Not one secret.

And then he waited.

So did the Voice, as if gathering evidence, weighing his confession, deliberating on a verdict.

There was enough to damn him for eternity. He saw that now. Accepted his fate.

At last the Judge on the ghastly throne spoke with the weight of eternal love. "I forgive you."

Just like that.

It didn't compute. The Pastor balked,

"But . . . but that was too easy."

Another long silence. The Pastor listened. And waited.

Silence—grave silence.

It seemed he waited for six hours or three days or all eternity.

And then the Voice said, "No, Son. No, it wasn't."

In that moment, he saw the Cross with new eyes, and the One hanging there—*perceived* at last what *He* had endured, absorbing every assault and assuming the Pastor's own fear, sickness, and perversion.

No, it was not easy, not at all.

Not easy at all for Jesus. He didn't *just* forgive.

He was crucified—humiliated, violated, tortured—and then He died.

No, not easy at all.

Then he heard Sage say, "No, Pastor. No. It wasn't."
A tear fell from her cheek.

And he saw Sage's life flash before him from beginning to end—the suffering he caused, the consequences and addictions she endured, the fear and hatred she bore because of him and for him, the battle she fought to overcome it.

No, it was not easy, not easy at all.
Not easy at all for Sage. She didn't *just* forgive.
She was sacrificed on the Pastor's pride and religion and abuse—crucified on his penis. She endured years of hell and fought for every step of her healing. And once whole, choosing to forgive required its own kind of death. A deeper death than one dies trying to escape—deeper and more powerful than death by drugs or suicide.

Death by forgiveness is a crucifixion, but she was willing.

And no, it was not easy. Not easy at all.

Nevertheless, not my will but Yours.

He saw it. And the Voice said, "And I will pour out a spirit of grace and prayer; and they will look on Me—the one they pierced. And they will mourn like one mourns losing an only child and will taste the bitterness of one who finds they've lost their firstborn."

And the Voice did just that. Godly sorrow flooded the Pastor's heart and mind. It poured in like a river and from his eyes and nose and pores. He wept bitterly, and mercifully, no one saw it on the monitors or interrupted to dam the healing flow.

Sage left him to it. "Let grief do its work," she said.

The grief continued. Waves of grief flooded over him for weeks on end—every morning he awoke and thought perhaps it was over, then a fresh wave would hit. When the grief abated—on the fortieth day—Sage visited again.

"Do you feel it now?" she asked. "Forgiven, I mean."

"Will I ever?" He was lying in his bed, and she propped his head up on a second pillow. No one took note.

"Yes. Here's the tangible evidence of forgiveness. It's when you think of what happened, and you're no longer afraid."

"That can happen? It seems impossible."

"It wasn't for me."

"What? How?"

"Pastor, I forgive you. I forgave you long ago."

"How? How is that possible? Why?"

"I wanted to be free. Free from the fear and rage that was killing me. I needed a Grace routine too, you know. The Good Book says to pray for our enemies. So, I began to pray for my enemy—for you—every day.

"At first I prayed every day that you'd be run over. Eventually, I prayed every day that I wouldn't run over you. There was a lot of silt in my well too. And then I took to praying that you wouldn't be run over, except by God. 'Vengeance is mine, I will repay,' he says. Okay, good. 'Repay away,' I said! I chose Christ and left the justice to him—trusted that he would do right by me.

"As for me, I was done. I could move on, 'let go and let God,' as they say. And when I did, the windows and doors flew open. Light poured in, light that flushed out fear and drained the anger. I let go, really let go, and I was free.

"But listen, Pastor. This is critical: the choice was mine. I could choose to forgive or not. I forgave, because I was forgiven. And when I forgave, freedom came. Freedom from anger and fear but also freedom *not* to contact you or any of my offenders. I was completely off your hook.

"But then I heard what happened, where you were. And I prayed, 'Lord, I could still hate that man if I *went there*—if I picked up the shackles again. No, thanks. So, I'm asking, have mercy on him, the same mercy you've shown me.'

"Of course, I didn't really mean it—not at first—but I said the words and tried not to relapse. And then one day, I had a meeting at the Cross—just like you. And I surrendered again—died another death. Grace offered me a choice, no strings attached, to midwife your healing.

"So, anyway, Pastor, I forgive you. I remember what you did, and I'm not afraid. That's my tangible proof. I'm free. And one day, I hope you'll be free too.

"So, this is my last visit. Keep up your Grace routine, and when it's time, Love will come."

"Your last visit?"

The old panic threatened to rise. Once, he could not bear to see her. The fear and shame were too much. Now, how could he bear to see her leave?

"Don't be afraid, Pastor. Love will visit you. Oh, one last thing, something I never thought I'd want or be able to do."

Sage drew close beside his bed and stretched her hand over his gown, just above his genitals. He was petrified.

"Oh God, I just knew it! Betrayed at last?"

"Still afraid, Pastor? It's okay. Remember, Love is coming. "

She didn't touch him, but as her hand began trembling, so did his legs. And between his legs, he felt a warmth, like oil—then heat and energy, coursing through him and over him. It continued for maybe ten minutes. Then Sage disappeared.

The Pastor's medical records would report that, from that day, his mutilation began mysteriously to heal.

Salvation

I DREAMED OF MAX.

He saved me. I know that sounds trite, like something the "born-agains" might say at a revival meeting.

But it isn't trite. You'll see.

First, Mallory reappeared.

She didn't touch me. Didn't even speak.

I got the sense she couldn't.

But she offered me a way out. An extension cord fastened to the ceiling.

And an idea. A choice.

I went so far as to wrap the extension cord around my neck, and I stood up on the edge of my bed. That's how I know I was dreaming—at least I think so. Whether in the body or out of the body, I don't really know—only Love knows.

I was done. Finished. Seconds from stepping off. It's traumatizing to think about how close I came. I shut my eyes, felt for the edge of the bed with my toes. And that's when I saw Max, standing before me—weeping.

Is there no good in me? I asked.

Here is what I saw in his eyes—what I saw in his tears.

"Yes, there is good in you. A treasure, in fact."
Somehow, I knew Max could not lie, and yet I knew I could not believe him.
I am a diaper. I am dirt.

I thought I confessed everything to Sage. I thought I was forgiven.
And now all this—these memories. I see no good thing in me. Not a single thing.

"You confessed every wrong you've done to others," Max replied. "You *are* forgiven. But these memories—they are wrongs done to you and the other children you loved so much. These wrongs left shards that pierce your soul to this day. They left sorrow and anger in you—along with all your judgments and determinations about them. These also need healing.

"Son, I love you as you are. I'll show you, if you'll allow me."

I wavered, diverted my look from the face of Love, reverted to my past and my flaws. I began to drift and isolate and strain at the cord.

I feel alone. I've failed everyone. I'm beyond hope. Who cares to hear this anymore?
How could I ever let you love me in this black hole?
Why are you here in my pit? You shouldn't be here.

"Son, I've been to hell and back. And I won. Now I wait in the darkest hell of your heart. For you. I've come to bring you back to life."

Life? Life has nothing for me. I don't want to come back. I have been in this cell for an eternity, in and out of sleep. I don't care whether I live or die. I just want to sleep and not wake up. Alone in the dark, it's so sweet and dangerous. I want to give up . . .
But I can't.

I looked up at Max. Those eyes.

I looked down at the edge of the bed. Vacillating.

I fought between listening to myself and seeing Max.

Every time I thought to end it, there was Max—weeping.

Finally, I burst into tears and stepped back.

Why are you crying?

"I weep with you, because I feel your pain—the pain of giving up. I weep for you, because you let me comfort you but won't let me heal you. Please, will you let me?"

Why do I resist?

"What you resist most is my complete acceptance of you. What will heal you is my complete acceptance of you."

Why does it hurt?

"The true and gentle fire of Love can feel like hell or like warmth and safety. It depends on whether you receive it or resist it. Look at me."

I peeked into the abyss and back into Max's eyes.

"What do you see?"

I see kindness and understanding and love and for-giveness. It should feel good, but it makes me want to run! I want it, but how can you feel that for me? It makes me crazy, and I don't know how to accept it. It feels like hell!

I closed my eyes again, locked them shut.

No. It's not for me! Your eyes are crushing me—crush-ing my heart.

"Better the crush of Love than the crush of your fa-ther's hate—and your self-hate. Don't be afraid. The fire you feel is not burning you. It is consuming what has been killing you—'all that is not of love's kind.' Keep gazing. Pain is nothing new to you, but healing is."

I knew Max was right. I opened my eyes, and this time, I refused to look away. Max's eyes began to draw out the pain, my past, and my self-hate—all the de-filement and corruption I carried—drew it out and into his eyes, dissolving it in love.

I can't look away. I won't let myself. I want you.

Max nodded. "That's right. Gaze and gaze and be cleaned and healed."

I did. I stared into Max's eyes, and I gazed and gazed. I was so broken; it was all I could do. Love took my shame, my blame, my self-hate. Drew it out with that look—into the eyes of Love.

He does love me. With all my flaws and all I've done to destroy myself.

He sees me, and he loves me. Me.

Max saved me.

Choice

DREAM OR NOT, it truly was a miracle.

But not just a miracle; it was *my choice*. When I wrapped myself in that cord, Love showed himself and gave me a choice. A real choice.

And I chose. I chose Love. I chose to live.

Best of all, Love didn't force me! Right down to those last seconds, it was my choice—continue on or step down into Love's arms. *My choice!*

It meant the world to me, because Love showed me we *all have* a choice! All of us. Including my father. It's not that Love *let* those horrible things happen to me. My father *chose* it! *They* chose it! *I chose it!*

This may sound strange, but it means I can trust him. I was never truly convinced before that God didn't play a part in what happened to me. Like maybe God let it happen to punish me for being dirty—for being a diaper.

But knowing Love—I can trust him now!

Since the dream, I keep gazing. It's part of my daily Grace routine. I picture Max's eyes—the eyes of love—and I feel safe and warm. The longer I gaze, the more heaviness is being lifted from me.

All my life, since I was old enough to have a memory of bits and pieces that I couldn't quite bury, I thought—no, I *knew*—I was bad and dirty. I just didn't know why. I didn't know what I had done to deserve what was happening.

And now I know it wasn't *me*! It wasn't me!

Love *never* saw me the way I saw myself. Love never saw me as filthy or dirty, disgraceful or vulgar. Love saw the diamond planted there from the start—pure and clear, innocent and beautiful.

Sometimes I dream of Max sitting and weeping for my pain. He wipes his tears on my face and over my body, and I feel the filth being brushed away, absorbed in his love. Each time I wake up, I feel clean, like I have fresh, new skin and new eyes to see what he has always seen in me. A son.

Sometimes I dream I'm leaning on Max's heart, and I let him love me. I actually *let* him—without walls or any distrust blocking the love. I feel warmth and comfort, but I can also feel Love. And safety. And a sense that this Love is *for me*. It's the purest thing I have ever felt.

And now I can trust Love. I'm willing. I'm not fighting Love anymore. It's so different now. I don't want to die anymore. I cry as I think about it. It's been so long since I could say that and know that I mean it. When I finally reached rock bottom, Love looked at me and gave me the courage to choose life. And now I don't want to hurt others or myself anymore.

I can let Love in.

I miss Max. I'm sad about what I did to him. I wish he were here. But maybe he visits my dreams to let me know I'm forgiven, even for that.

Love

"And then Love roared.
Louder than my demons."

MAX?

The Pastor had been dreaming of Max again.

Not lifeless Max with the broken neck but faithful Max—his patient and faithful companion, very much alive.

Not puppy-dog Max who always seemed underfoot. But ever-present guardian Max—watchful, discerning.

Not even Max the mute amputee—the Max of his dreams could speak and write and put his right hand on his shoulder. Or his heart.

"Maximos," he had said in the dream. "My friends call me Maximos."

"Maximos. May I call you that too?"

"Of course. I'm your friend, aren't I?"

In the dream, Maximos placed his hand on the Pastor's heart and gave him a fatherly blessing—just one word: "Son." A blessing of identity he'd never received from his own "sire." Max could see the Pastor's true self and help him see it too.

The moment he felt that hand, the Pastor's mouth opened wide—it felt like his jaw might dislocate. That moment of silence when a child is about to wail but has not yet gathered a breath for the blast.

And then a deep howl burst from the Pastor's mouth—in the dream and in his cell, breaking through the shell of his coma and through his cell door and down every hall of the ward. The firetruck-siren howl broke every blood vessel in his face and neck—brought orderlies and nurses scurrying. This was the first peep he'd made in their memory. It was deafening—alarming.

In his dream—now a waking vision—he felt himself levitate, his feet and legs floating behind him. But his gaze was glued to Max's determined, caring eyes— the most beautiful thing he'd ever seen.

Before the ward staff could administer a sedative, the Pastor's cry had subsided, and he lapsed back into catatonic stillness. They puzzled and murmured and updated his chart and finally let him be, his bed adjusted to a sitting position.

But Maximos was still there, his hand on his heart.

The Pastor's initial eruption had been a reaction to the jolt of overwhelming power—the love he felt touching him, entering his heart from Maximos' palms. The sudden impact hit like a cattle prod. Now it felt like pure comfort, thick, sweet honey, and he hoped it would never stop.

He could only whisper to Maximos, *Stay?*

"Always."

And that's when he recognized Him.

THIS WAS NO DREAM. On his bed. As with the visitations of Mallory and Sage, the Pastor could hear with his ears, see with his eyes, feel the touch of Maximos' hand—unobservable to anyone else but fully tangible for him.

She said Love would come. Sage, I mean.

"She did. And I have."

It's You.

"Yes, son."

Thank you. Just . . . thank you. You'll really stay?

"Always. But especially now. You've been through much, but there's still a dark valley to traverse. But don't be afraid. I'll go with you, guide you, and I won't leave your side—not for a moment—even if you lose sight of me."

I've got a bad feeling about this.

"It will be hard. But remember, not rock hard, only ice hard."

Maximos slid beside the Pastor onto the bed. "We'll make the entire journey from here, son."

He took the Pastor's head in his hands and pulled it tight to his own heart. With his strong right hand, he stroked the Pastor's hair as if he were a child, invoking sobs from deep below the Pastor's conscious mind. With each wave came memories like those of his dreams. Images from before his first wound, those brief years of innocence. Memories of the precise moment of his first deep wound. The blindside of childhood betrayal. The awful growing aftermath— repeated hurt and harm, snowballing consequences, violent fantasies, obsessions and compulsions. And the darkness of his choice for control, infecting his conversion and call to ministry, even while pushing his past down into the dark abyss of denial.

Still, Maximos held him, his touch reminding the boy he was not alone.

Awake

I sleep, but my heart is awake;
I heard the voice of my beloved!
He knocks: "Open for me, my sister,
my love, my dove, my perfect one . . ."
—Song of Songs

I baptize you with water for repentance.
But after me comes one who is more powerful than
I, whose sandals I am not worthy to carry. He will
baptize you with the Holy Spirit and fire.
—St John the Forerunner

I WAS ASLEEP, BUT MY HEART WAS AWAKE.

Then Love spoke, but not with words.

I lay there, still in exile from the external world, enclosed and impenetrable in my unresponsive body.

But I faithfully practiced the Grace routine Sage had given me.

1. Wake up
2. Pee (Thank you, Lord, for catheters.)
3. Listen
4. Surrender

And one day, Love visited me and gave me a vision—no, more than a vision. An experience.

At first, I felt the encounter was just for me—a secret between Love and me.

But I feel kind of mind blown, and I need to profess it. Someone—maybe you—needs to hear about it, about my vision/experience. So, with an open heart, I share Love's visit with you, hoping you can hear me and maybe make it your own.

After praying—I only trust myself to pray three words: *Lord, have mercy*—I listened. And the eyes of my heart were opened. I looked down and saw layers of my body blackening. They decomposed and became fragile—as brittle as ash—and fell away.

Suddenly, my entire body ignited—burst into flames. But rather than scorching me, it felt refreshing. Then I felt a fresh wind gust over me, from head to toe—a catalyst for release—blowing away the loose layers of ash.

This seems familiar. I remembered Moses at the

mountain of God—Horeb, which means waste or desert. That describes me well, don't you think? Then Moses saw the burning bush—ablaze but not consumed.

I didn't have to think about it. I just knew Grace was baptizing me—baptizing me with fire. The fire was washing me—not just the dirt on the outside but purging the filth on the inside. First with fire. Then with pure water—sprinkling my heart, cleansing my guilty conscience, washing my body.

After everything was burned up and blown away and washed off, I saw myself. Where the ashen shell had been was a tiny baby—me, with pink skin, fresh and clean and new.

The fire of Love not only washed away my old, dead self; Love had uncovered my first self, my true self, my new and renewed self—a fresh body, a fresh mind, and a fresh soul.

I had passed through the fiery judgment, but it was not what I thought.

I used to preach about hell a lot—about God's wrath, the furnace of fire and brimstone, the wicked burning in torment for all eternity. I even used the burning bush to say God would burn the wicked without consuming them. That way, their punishment would persist without relief forever. I reveled in their wailing and gnashing, because "they" deserved it—no, because *I deserved it.*

I projected my self-loathing onto God as the angry punisher, and my "calling" was to terrify people into repentance. My "ministry" was a toxic expression of my own self-hatred. My moral outrage was a self-defeating coping mechanism, a kind of confession where I vomited on others from the rot in my own heart and guts. I knew whatever hell was, it was for me, so I preached that it was for "them."

Sick? I know.

I did that.

Yet, when Love appears to Moses as fire, I don't see punishment.

And in my vision, the Fire I once interpreted as hell is fierce Love, the very means of my inner healing. The Fire speaks of the enormity, the depth, and the vastness of divine love and grace, mercy, and forgiveness. Love is the fiery furnace I underwent in the vision.

I can feel it in my bones that Christ didn't just die on the Cross for me long ago at a single point in time.

It's as if the Cross stands over time and through time—"the Lamb slain from all eternity"—and all creation flows from the wound in his side.

I saw the slain Lamb waiting patiently to be *my* Lamb.

I saw what he suffered with me and for me to show me this:

The Lamb loves me,
Has always loved me,
Will love me forever.

And if the Lamb loves *me* that way, would he withhold his love from you?

If Love found me, could it overlook you?

If Grace pursued even me, will she ever turn from you?

I used to see the Cross as a badge of my belief or a talisman of spiritual protection. Now I see that *the Cross is the fire* of God's unwavering love and scandalous forgiveness. It summons me to show others the same mercy God showed me—that Sage showed me. Love asks *me* to be the unconsumed bush, burning with the unquenchable fire of Love, day by day, moment by moment. To *become* the fire and embody the love as Sage did.

Yes, I passed through the fires of hell—we all do. But my great awakening came when I saw the flames that engulfed me were relentless Love.

I stood condemned in the courtroom of my own self-judgment. Fair enough, I suppose—if it were about "fair." But I failed to see the possibility of self-forgiveness and self-acceptance. I rejected mercy and grace as "too easy."

In truth, what was I asking?
"Am I worthy of love?"
The answer had always been a resounding "No!"

~ ~ ~ ~ ~

WHEN LOVE VISITED my dreams and the healing Fire came, I felt that cool sensation wash through my entire body and soul. It consumed my apprehension and distrust. And now I know:

God is good and merciful and the Lover of humankind.

Grace has forgiven me; the fear is gone, and Love has come.

And I am perfectly alright.

Here in this hospital cell—my hermitage—I continue my program, one day at a time.

1. Wake up (I see him)
2. Pee (Thank you, Lord.)
3. Listen, "Lord, have mercy . . ."

"He spoke! Oh my god! He spoke!" the orderly shouted. "Nurse! Quick! Call the nurse!"

"What? What is it?"

"It's the patient! He's awake!
. . . Jesus Christ, he's awake!"

Bradley Jersak

While Bradley Jersak is not "the Pastor" in this novel, he has faced the reality of his own ministry meltdown. Twelve years into his healing journey, he enjoys the goodness of waking up to God's unfailing love.

His written works include theology, political science, spirituality and children's books, including *Jesus Showed Us*. *The Pastor* is his first fiction title. Brad now serves as Dean of Theology & Culture at St. Stephen's University (New Brunswick). He and his wife Eden live in Abbotsford, Canada.

Paul Young

Wm. Paul Young, Canadian author of the novels, *The Shack, Cross Roads,* and *Eve,* and non-fiction *Lies We Believe about God,* was raised among a stone-age tribe by his missionary parents in the highlands of what was Netherlands New Guinea (now West Papua). He suffered great loss as a child and young adult, and now enjoys the "wastefulness of grace" with his growing family in the Pacific Northwest.

Facts never tell real stories and also do not speak to the potency of love and forgiveness, the arduous road of reconciliation, the surprises of grace and community, of transformational healing and the unexpected emergence of joy.